TIMBUCTOO
CLUCK

A sort of hen from Timbuctoo

a story by
Roger Hargreaves

© Mrs Roger Hargreaves 1999
Published in Great Britain by Egmont World Ltd.,
Deanway Technology Centre, Wilmslow Road, Handforth,
Cheshire, SK9 3FB.
Printed in Italy
ISBN PBK 0 7498 4348 9
ISBN HBK 0 7498 4418 3

CLUCK was a sort of hen.
A not very clever hen.
A Timbuctoo Hen.

She lived in Nest Cottage,
on the island of Timbuctoo.

Hens, as you know, are not particularly clever, and **CLUCK** was probably Less Clever Than Any Hen You've Ever Met.

One fine morning she was sitting in her kitchen, in Nest Cottage, having breakfast ...

cornflake sandwiches ...

when there was a knock at the door.

KNOCK KNOCK KNOCK!

"That," thought **CLUCK**, "sounds like a knock at the door."

So she went to the door, and opened it.

The oven door!

"Whoops!" said **CLUCK**.

WHOOOOOOOPPPPPPS!

And went to the window, and opened that!

As we said earlier, **CLUCK** was not the cleverest hen in the world!

It was **OINK** the Timbuctoo Postman.

"Good morning!" cried **CLUCK**, through the window.

"Two pints, please!"

"I'm not the milkman, you silly hen," said Oink. "I'm a postman, and I have a letter for you."

"Oooo," said **CLUCK**, for she didn't often get letters.

"Oooo! I wonder who it's from?"

"Well," said Oink. "There's only one way to find out!"

OOOOOOOOOOOO!

"And what," asked **CLUCK**, through the window, "might that be?"

"Why – open it, of course," laughed Oink.

"Oh yes," said **CLUCK**. "I hadn't thought of that. Thank you, milkman!"

Oink shook his head, and went on his way.

HA HA HA HA HA HA!

CLUCK took the letter and sat down at the kitchen table.

"Now," she thought. "How exactly does one go about opening a letter?"

She propped the letter against the teapot, and sat there looking at it.

She couldn't think how to open it!

CLUCKKKKKKKKKKKKK!

"If," she thought, "I was opening a door, I'd turn the handle."

She picked up the letter and examined it.

Very carefully.

"No handle," she said.

"If," she thought, "I was opening a window, I'd push it."

So she picked up the letter, and pushed it across the table.

HOW??????????

"Hmm!" she thought.

"What works with windows does not necessarily work with letters."

CLUCK sat looking at the letter, and thinking.

She had another cornflake sandwich to help her to think.

"Life is a problem," she sighed as she picked up the cornflake sandwich and took a bite.

"Ugh!" she spluttered. "Ugh!"

You see, **CLUCK** was thinking so hard, she'd picked up the letter as well as the sandwich. And, instead of taking a bite of the sandwich, she had taken a bite of the letter!

And, by taking a bite out of the letter, instead of the sandwich, she'd actually opened it.

"Remarkable," chuckled **CLUCK**.

Inside the envelope, with a bite out of it, was a long letter from **NEIGH**.

Neigh was a sort of horse, who was a sort of friend of **CLUCK'S**.

CLUCK sat in her favourite armchair.

She looked at Neigh's long letter.

"I wish I could read," she said.